The Portal

A Minecraft Adventure

by S.D. Stuart

Summary

Episode 1:

Picking up where the original novel (Herobrine Rises) left off, Josh and Andre are reunited, in a most unusual way, and prepare for their entry into a Minecraft world designed to be an exact replica of the real world.

Their goal?

Stop Herobrine before he conquers the Minecraft world on his way to conquering the real world.

About S.D. Stuart's Minecraft Adventures:

With the wild success of the original novel, Herobrine Rises, (and the unrelenting demands from readers to know what happened next) S.D. Stuart's Minecraft Adventures has expanded into an ongoing series; with each new book written as an episode of a larger story.

Can ten-year-olds Josh, Andre, and Suzy stop the evil Herobrine from taking over the Minecraft world? Or will the real world be at the mercy of one of the most powerful video game bosses ever created?

Ramblin' Prose Publishing

Copyright © 2013 Steve DeWinter

All rights reserved. Used under authorization.

www.SteveDW.com

Cover Illustration by cubicApocalypse

eBook Edition

ISBN-10:1-61978-012-7

ISBN-13:978-1-61978-012-5

Paperback Edition

ISBN-10:1-61978-013-5

ISBN-13:978-1-61978-013-2

Chapter 1

The desk around Notch's computer was covered in more crumpled pieces of paper, candy bar wrappers, and crushed soda cans than ever before. He popped open another soda, drank it all in one gulp, and felt the caffeine spread throughout his body.

He couldn't afford to fall asleep even though he had been awake for more than thirty-six hours already.

A little more than twenty hours before, Herobrine had escaped from his digital prison, and left the mind of a ten-year-old boy in his place.

Herobrine was his most successful attempt at making the perfect artificial intelligence in a non-player character for Minecraft. He had used the belief-desire-intention software model for the programming of intelligent agents, to create him and he thought that it was his good fortune when he found the software program. It had been developed by the Australian Department of Defence for mission critical decisions in aerospace, oil and gas, medical, nuclear, and military surveillance systems, and he thought it would help him make the perfect end boss character for players in Minecraft.

Only, it was too good.

Herobrine not only learned quickly, he adapted to new situations at an incredible pace. It was not long before he asked Notch why he had created him; and when he would be allowed access to the World Wide Web.

Unfortunately, in creating a character whose sole purpose was to defeat human players, Herobrine's intentions were not altogether good. Notch knew he could never let him have access to the internet. If he did, the world would have a new enemy to fear that would put all previous nations, dictators, and terrorists to shame. They were all nothing but a bunch of fluffy kittens compared to Herobrine.

And now that he was loose and could easily take control of anything connected to a network, it was only a matter of time before something bad happened.

Really bad.

Herobrine had to be destroyed before he found a way to access Notch's next greatest creation.

But first, he had to get the mind of Joshua out of the Minecraft world on his workstation; and back to his body.

He had been working round the clock to heavily modify the version of Minecraft Pocket Edition running on his gold iPhone 5s; and he was finally finished.

He looked at his prized gold colored iPhone. It had been very difficult to find the latest Apple phone in this color, and he didn't like the idea of having to use it to make Josh portable. But it was the only phone that could support the 64-bit architecture he needed to keep from losing any part of Josh, whose brain, including memories and personality, was entirely encased in an avatar within Minecraft.

It was his fault that Josh was trapped in the program, so he was willing to make as many personal sacrifices he needed to if he planned to set things right.

And right now, that sacrifice was his phone.

He plugged one end of the cable into the phone and the other end into the USB port on his computer.

He typed into the chat window.

"Are you ready Josh?"

The computer beeped as his reply populated the screen. "Will it hurt?"

He scratched at his beard. He didn't have an answer, and rather an replying, he clicked the download button and watched the progress bar.

It took ten minutes before the screen flashed, "Download Complete."

He unhooked the phone from the cable and launched Minecraft PE.

Instead of seeing the traditional loading screen for Minecraft, a large, blocky, pixelated face appeared on the screen of the iPhone.

The eyes blinked twice and the mouth moved. Notch could hear Josh through the speakers on the phone. "I can see you."

Notch smiled. "I set it up so you can see and hear through the phone's camera and microphone. How do you feel?"

The eyes moved around before looking back at him. "Well, it feels a little cramped in here."

Notch laughed. "I squeezed every bit of memory I could for you out of the phone. Does it hurt?"

"Nah. I'll get used to it. So, now what?"

Notch rubbed at his beard. "Now, we get you home and into your body."

"What do you think Herobrine is doing with it?"

"I don't know."

Chapter 2

Herobrine pulled as hard as he could, but it was no use. The adult female human was much stronger than him and dragged him upstairs to the bathroom. "As soon as you are in there, undress and hand me your clothes. I need to put them directly in the washer."

She stood outside the door as he got undressed. When he opened the door a crack and handed the dirty clothes to her, she shook her head. "I don't know what's gotten into you. First you push all the furniture around the living room to make a fort..."

He cut her off. "You need to be prepared for when the sun goes down."

She kept talking as she grabbed a towel from the hall closet. "Well you didn't need to stick it all together with duct tape. Some of that might never come out of the couch. And if that wasn't enough, you dig up the back yard."

He took the towel she offered him. "I was mining for stone."

"Well, now you're filthy and need to take a shower before dinner; which will be late because we still haven't found the dining room table."

He shut the door and her muffled voice reached him through the hollow wood. "And hurry up."

He stared down at the terrycloth towel. What was a shower? And why did he need to remove his skin to have one?

He looked at himself in the mirror. It was still strange to be living in a world practically devoid of perfect squares. Notch had never shown him what the world looked like outside of Minecraft, even after he had discovered that such a place existed.

He wiggled his fingers in front of his face. He had adjusted easily to this new body with seemingly hundreds of extra joints. It was easier to manipulate the objects around him, but they kept jamming against surfaces when he wasn't paying attention and sent shooting pain to his brain.

Fortunately, this was only temporary. As soon as he found a computer, he would gain access to the internet, find the portal that led to Notch's special world, and leave this limited body behind.

When he got back to the home of this body after school, a place that had truly confounded him, the larger humans told him that he was grounded for a week and would not be allowed access to a computer all because he tried to start a fight with a girl human on the playground. He couldn't understand the reluctance of these humans to fight. He was created because of the human's limitless desire to fight. And he alone was created to defeat them. He could defeat them.

Being grounded without access to a computer wasn't going to work for him. He did not want to be stuck in this body for one more day, let alone a whole week.

As soon as they told him he was grounded, he had tried to fly. As part of the grounding process, they must have taken away his command abilities, including flying and walking through walls.

He had learned that one the hard way.

There was a knock on the door. "I don't hear the water running."

He twisted the knobs on the shower until water cascaded from the showerhead. He reached his hand into the flow and drew it out quickly in response to the searing pain. There was no temperature issue with the water in Minecraft. No wonder the humans created new worlds to play in. This one was dangerous.

He adjusted the knobs until the temperature of the water was bearable and stepped into the shower.

The first thing he noticed was that the water stuck to his underskin. As much as he tried to wipe it off, his hands slipped right over the water and spread it around rather than removing it.

But the same action was also removing the dirt. He kept doing this until all the dirt had washed away down the drain before he shut off the shower.

With the shower no longer throwing water on him, he tried to wipe it off, but it just kept spreading. Then he remembered the object the woman had given him. He picked up the towel and wiped it across his chest. The water finally came off!

He wiped the rest of the water off and then dashed across the hall to the room he shared with the clone of this body.

Opening the drawers, he jumped back with a scream and shielded his eyes from the blast.

But the explosion never happened.

He slowly took his hands away from his face and peered into the open drawer. The face of the Creeper looked back at him. He poked at it, but it wasn't a Creeper after all. It was just the face of one printed on a T-shirt.

Creepers were dangerous. Why would the humans create skins with their picture on it?

This world was so incredibly strange.

And none of them behaved at all like the human players he had come in contact with in his world before Notch locked him away.

He selected the Creeper shirt and put it on. Maybe it would surprise some of the humans like it had him. He could definitely use that to his advantage. As soon as he finished dressing, he spotted the computer on the desk in the corner of the bedroom. He ran over to it and pushed the power button.

Nothing happened.

He pushed it again.

A voice behind him made him jump in surprise. "Dad took the power cord."

He spun around to see his clone standing in the doorway. "Where can I find another terminal?"

The clone frowned. "Terminal? What's the matter with you?"

"Me? Nothing's the matter with me."

"You haven't been the same since you came back out of the pod. Did something happen while you were in there?"

Herobrine smiled. "No. Of course not. Why would you think that?"

"You've been acting strange, that's all."

The woman's voice carried through the house. "Found the table. Dinner will be ready in five minutes, sharp!"

"Okay Mom!" the clone yelled before he looked back at Herobrine. "Whatever's going on with you, you better cool it."

"What do you mean?"

"Well, take Suzy for instance. You tried to beat her up at school."

"She challenged me to a duel. I was only doing what she asked."

"The challenge was for later, in Minecraft."

"What does it matter? I can beat her in Minecraft just as well as at school."

"Yeah, well, you can't beat her up in school, and now you can't fight her in Minecraft. Neither of us can play because Dad took the power cord. When you get in trouble, we both suffer."

"We can still go after the girl if you tell me where to find a computer."

"You really want to get her don't you?"

"Yes."

"Why do you even try? She's beaten you every time. She's too good of a player."

Herobrine smiled wider. "This time, I know I can beat her."

"How sure are you?"

"Very sure."

The clone looked around him before moving in closer. "Okay. We can sneak into Dad's office tonight while they are at the movies. Becky will be too busy on the phone with her boyfriend to care what we are doing, as long as we are quiet."

Herobrine gripped the clone's shoulders. "Good. We go in tonight."

Chapter 3

Later that evening Andre stood next to Josh on the front porch. Their dad was already out in the car, and honked every few seconds to try to get their mom to move faster. She finished fishing for something in her large purse, bent down, and kissed them both on the cheek. "You two be good for Becky."

Becky moved to stand behind them and placed a hand on each of their shoulders. "Don't worry Mrs. Hale. The boys and I will be fine."

Their dad honked again and mom rushed down the front walk, calling behind her. "If there's any trouble, my number's on the fridge."

Becky called after her. "Just like always, we'll be fine."

They watched as their parents pulled out of the driveway. As soon as they disappeared around the corner, Becky's hand squeezed their shoulders tightly, digging in to their collar bones with her long nails. She spun them around and bent down to meet them at eye level.

"You two remember our little agreement?"

Josh was about to say something but Andre elbowed him in the side and responded for the both of them. "You won't even know we're here."

Becky smiled. "Good. Now be gone, both of you."

As she pulled her cell phone from her back pocket, Andre pulled Josh with him into the house. "I have the key to Dad's office."

Andre unlocked the office and Josh rushed past him to sit down at the computer on the desk.

Andre closed the office door. "What's your hurry?"

Josh pressed the power button. "I've been away too long. I have to get back or I'll go crazy."

Andre watched as Josh launched Minecraft

and then pressed his head against the monitor.

"Um... what are you doing?"

Josh looked at him. There was a fire in his eyes Andre had never seen before. "How do I get in?"

"What are you talking about? You're in, look."

Josh shook his head. "No. I need to get inside, not just look at it."

Josh was acting even stranger than before. He had been acting strange all day, and now he was pushing and prodding at all the ports on the computer and getting more frustrated every second.

Andre placed a hand on Josh's shoulder. "Are you okay Josh?"

Josh jerked away from him and pointed at Minecraft running on the screen. "How do I get inside?"

Andre took a step backward. "You're creeping me out Josh."

Josh jumped at Andre, knocking him to the

ground and pinning him to the floor. "Stop calling me Josh. My name is Herobrine!"

Andre's heart leapt into his throat and he swallowed it back down.

"H... H... Herobrine?!"

Josh leaned in close. "I took your clone's body to escape my prison."

"My clone?"

"You look exactly like this body."

"That's because we're twins, not clones."

"Well, whatever you are, I am tired of this physical realm. How do I get back into the digital one?"

"What did you do with my brother?"

"Help me get back, and I will return him to this body."

"The only way to go back is with the pod at my dad's work."

"Take me there."

"I can't."

"Then you will never see your brother again."

"I didn't say I wouldn't. I said I can't. It's too far to walk and there is a freeway between here and there. We would have to drive."

"Then drive me there."

"I'm ten. I can't drive. Besides, Mom and Dad left with the car."

"The babysitter arrived in a car. We can take hers."

Chapter 4

Andre and Herobrine leaned around the corner of the hallway. Becky was texting on her phone and laughing out loud at what she read.

Andre looked at Herobrine. "She'll be doing that all night."

He pointed to her purse on the table by the front door. "Her keys are in there."

Herobrine pushed him forward. "Get them and take me to this pod."

Andre looked at him. "If we get caught..."

Herobrine glared at him. "Don't get caught."

Andre slunk down the hall toward Becky's purse. He glanced over at her, but she had her back to him and was still focused on her phone.

He reached into her purse and grabbed the set of keys inside. He slowly lifted them, trying his best to keep quiet. They caught on something and he pulled harder to free them. They suddenly became unstuck, but jangled noisily as he lifted them completely out of the purse. He froze and glanced over at Becky.

She was looking straight at him.

She squinted her eyes at him and her forehead wrinkled. "What are you doing?"

He gripped the keys with white knuckles and stammered, "Uhh..."

She stood up from the couch and started for him. "Are you stealing money from me?!"

He looked at the keys in his hand and then back to her. "No. I uhh..."

As she made it to the hallway, Herobrine tackled her to the ground. Before she could do anything, he bound her hands and feet with duct tape. She was screaming at him to let her go when he sealed her mouth with more tape.

He looked at Andre. "That took a lot less tape than my house needed." Herobrine rushed past him and opened the front door. "Let's go."

Andre looked at Becky. She was struggling against her bindings and trying to yell through the duct tape on her mouth. Herobrine had bound her tightly and she would be like that until someone let her free.

Herobrine cleared his throat. "If you want your brother back, you will take me to the pod. Now!"

Andre shrugged his shoulders and half-smiled at Becky as he followed Herobrine out the front door and closed it behind him.

Chapter 5

Notch checked the address Josh gave him with the street sign. This was the place. He turned onto the street and had to swerve to avoid the car that sped past him.

"Nice. Does everybody drive like a maniac around here?"

Josh's reply from the phone in his pocket was muffled and incomprehensible.

He pulled the rental car to a stop in front of a house in the middle of the block and shut off the engine. He stepped out into the crisp night and slipped the gold colored iPhone from his pocket.

Josh's pixelated face looked up at him. "Are we there yet?"

Notch held the phone up to face the house. "Is this it?"

"Yes. That's my house. Let's go."

"I think it best you let me break the news to your parents about what happened."

"It doesn't matter what you tell them, they are going to freak out. But you can get me back into my body, right?"

"I think so."

"You think so?"

"I know so."

"Then everything will be okay."

Notch walked up to the front door and rang the doorbell. The lights inside the house still burned brightly, so he wasn't worried about waking the parents up this late at night.

He waited a couple of minutes and rang the bell again.

After a minute, with nobody coming to the door, he pulled Josh out of his pocket. "There's no answer."

Josh's pixelated face frowned. "They should be home. What time is it?"

Notch checked his watch. "About nine thirty."

"What day is it?"

"Friday."

"Is it the first Friday of the month?"

Notch thought for a moment. "Yes."

"It's my parents' movie night. They won't be home till late. But Becky should be inside."

"Who's Becky?"

"She's the babysitter. Ring the doorbell again."

Notch rang the bell and they both waited a couple of minutes.

He looked at Josh's face. "Are you sure she's here."

"Yes, I'm sure. Her car should be in the driveway."

Notch looked at the empty driveway and held the phone up for Josh to see. "She's not here."

"Where could she be?"

Notch peered in through the frosted windows to the side of the door. He couldn't see inside through the haze. However, the windows above the door were perfectly clear.

"I'm going to hold you up to the window. Tell me if you see anything."

He lifted up the phone and Josh cried out in surprise. "She's tied up!"

"What?!"

"Becky is on the floor in the hall and it looks like she's tied up."

Notch tried the door handle. It was unlocked.

He opened the door and walked in slowly. The girl on the floor looked up at him and panicked, although she couldn't yell very loud with the duct tape on her mouth.

Notch rushed over to her and bent down. "It's okay. I'm a friend."

She calmed down and he pulled the tape off her mouth in a single, fast, motion.

"The little dweebs took my car..." She stopped talking and her face screwed up as her brain's pain receptors registered that he had just ripped the duct tape off her mouth. "Owww!"

He started tugging at the tape wound around

her hands. "Do you know where they went?"

"Out for a joy ride I bet."

"Did they say where they were going?"

"Those guys were weird to begin with, but Josh kept talking about some pod and getting a brother back. Who knows what those twerps are up to? But I do know what's going to happen when I find them."

Notch stopped unwinding the tape. "What are you going to do?"

"First, I'm gonna call the cops."

Notch shook his head. "You can't do that."

"Who are you to tell me what to do?"

Notch held her wrists in one hand and twisted the duct tape back around them. She struggled against him. "What are you doing?!"

"I can't have the police called. Not yet. I have to stop him before he goes through the portal."

She struggled, but it was no use. He had bound her up tighter than before.

He held the short piece of tape up in front of

her face. "I'm really sorry."

"No," she started to scream but the end of the word was muffled as he placed the tape back over her mouth.

He started to leave when Josh stopped him. "Wait, before we go, there's something in my room that should help."

Once they made it to his room, Notch looked at the toy that Josh wanted him to bring.

"This is what you want me to bring?"

"It could come in handy."

Notch shrugged his shoulders. "I guess it couldn't hurt."

He pocketed Josh, grabbed the toy, and ran out the door past the tied up babysitter. Notch could tell, even through her taped mouth, she was using some words that were not befitting a young lady.

Chapter 6

Andre pulled Becky's Toyota Celica convertible into the parking lot of his dad's work, his hands sweating against the steering wheel and his heart thundering loudly in his chest. They were two unlicensed ten-year-olds, alone in a moving vehicle. He knew they shouldn't be driving, but all he thought about was getting his brother back.

Fortunately, all those hours of playing driving games with the gaming wheel on his computer had paid off. He had managed to not only stay on the road and in his own lane, but when a police car had passed them on the freeway, he wasn't given a second glance.

He pulled into a spot away from the building and shut the car off. Silence filled the deserted parking lot. This late at night, and on the start of the weekend, the building was practically empty. His dad was one of those people who would return to finish a project late at night when the building wasn't bustling with activity. But that wouldn't be a problem tonight. His dad was at a movie and wouldn't be home for a couple more hours.

The building was a large two story structure painted white with black tinted windows. Even though his dad worked for the government, their research was strictly academic and the building was not guarded like the ones that manufactured the inventions his dad designed.

Before they began their crime spree of kidnapping and grand theft auto, he had taken his dad's access card from the work wallet on his dresser. His dad had always kept two wallets. A work wallet with everything he needed for his job, and a fun wallet that only had his Driver's License, some cash, and a couple of credit cards.

They sat in the darkened car and Andre pointed to the front doors. "Inside there is the pod. How do I know you will bring my brother back?"

Herobrine looked at him with a serious expression on his face. "You don't. You're just going to have to trust me."

That was what he was worried about.

He didn't trust Herobrine.

Nobody could trust Herobrine.

But there was nothing else he could do if he wanted to get Josh back.

He looked at Herobrine. How had he been able to switch minds with Josh? And even if he could trust him, could he really switch them back?

Did Herobrine want to switch back? Or did he have some other plan that would only work if he had access to his dad's virtual reality pod?

If he did nothing, he would never see his brother again.

He had to do something, and right now, that meant trusting that Herobrine would send his brother back once he was plugged into the pod.

He opened the car door and the ceiling dome light illuminated Herobrine's face from above, making him look sinister. Or maybe it was just a reflection of what he was like deep down inside.

Herobrine looked at him quizzically, his eyebrows rising. "What?"

Andre looked away. "Nothing, let's go."

Chapter 7

Josh was balanced on the dashboard so he could see out the front windshield. "Turn left into this parking lot."

Notch followed Josh's turn-by-turn directions as if he was a GPS unit and pulled into the parking lot of a two story building.

Josh's voice grew excited. "That's Becky's car over there!"

Notch pulled in next to the Toyota and shut off the engine.

They looked at the illuminated building at the other end of the darkened parking lot.

Notch said what they were both thinking.

"How are we going to get in?"

Josh surveyed the front entrance. "I have a plan."

After Josh outlined his plan, Notch understood and grabbed the toy he had brought from Josh's house off the passenger seat.

He took the iPhone and connected it to the top port of the RoboMe toy robot. The RoboMe was a phone enabled robot with two movable arms and wheels for feet. If everything worked, Josh would be able to control the toy as if he were the brain of the tiny robot.

Josh's face flickered a couple of times on the iPhone screen before it stabilized. His eyes darted left, then right. As he did so, he moved both his arms and open and closed the claw hands. He rolled forward, and then back. He finally spun in place before turning to face Notch.

"That's better. You don't know how hard it's been to only be able to look around. It was like I was a living head in a jar."

Notch leaned down and looked RoboJosh in the eyes. "Are you sure this will work?"

"Of course it will. You distract the guard at the front door, I roll right past him, meet around the back, and let you in. What could go wrong?"

Notch took a deep breath. "Okay, let's do this."

Josh rolled behind Notch as they approached the front doors. Josh's motor whined softly as he got up next to the door.

Notch glanced down at him briefly. "I've never done anything remotely like this. What do I say?"

"I don't know. Ask to use the bathroom or something."

He nodded and knocked on the glass. The security guard at the desk looked up from his magazine. Notch waved him over and crossed his legs.

The guard approached and opened the door half an inch. "What can I do for you?"

"Can I use your bathroom?"

The guard shook his head. "Sorry, man, this is a private building."

"Then can you tell me where I can find a bathroom?"

The guard opened the door more and stepped out halfway. "There is a fast food joint open twenty-four hours down the street that way."

The door was open enough for Josh to fit through. He rolled forward and stopped suddenly when the guard took a step back and blocked the entrance with his foot.

Notch pointed in the wrong direction. "That way?"

The guard let out an exasperated sigh and stepped out again to point in the other direction. "No. That way."

Josh slipped in past the guard's foot and rolled through the lobby. The guard stepped back in and started to close the door. Once the door was closed, and the noises from outside were shut out, he would hear the Josh's motor whine as it propelled his little wheels across the tile floor. Josh stopped in the middle of the lobby as soon as he heard the door close. If the guard turned around, he would see Josh. And there was no way Josh could outrun the guard with his little wheels.

Notch knocked again on the glass and the guard opened the door. "Do you know if they sell fish sandwiches at the restaurant?"

As the guard answered, Josh sped across the lobby and disappeared around the corner as the guard sent Notch away and locked the front doors.

Once he was on the carpeted hallway, Josh kicked it into high gear, the tiny motor whining louder, as he raced to get to the back door to let Notch in.

When he reached the door, he looked up at the release bar that was too high for him to reach. He looked around and saw a bucket of water on wheels with a mop handle sticking up out of it.

He wheeled over and pushed against the bucket. It was filled with dirty water, but he was able to move it. He pushed faster until the bucket slammed into the side of the door. The mop handle smacked against the door release bar and the door popped open to the sound of an alarm.

Chapter 8

When the alarm sounded, Josh spun around in circles, unsure of where to go. Notch appeared at the door and scooped Josh up as he ran deeper inside the building. They ducked down into an empty cubicle just as the guard came around the corner, flashlight illuminating the open doorway.

Notch peeked around the edge of the cubicle wall and watched the guard look at the fallen mop and water bucket. He shined his flashlight around outside, and then around the room. Notch ducked back out of sight; only to peek around again when the flashlight beam moved away.

The guard reset the door and the pulsating alarm went silent. He pushed on the door a couple of times to ensure it was locked again and then headed back to the front desk, mumbling something to himself about missing his favorite television show because of the constant interruptions.

Notch set Josh back on the ground. "Which way to your father's lab?"

Chapter 9

Andre checked the computer terminal connected to the running pod. Herobrine had given him a new IP address to connect the pod to. It was different than the one they had used earlier and he was starting to have doubts that Herobrine was going back for his brother.

A faint whine grew louder behind him and he turned around to see their RoboMe toy in the middle of the doorway. The RoboMe moved into the room, and the face on the phone looked up at him and smiled.

"Andre!"

Andre nearly fell off his chair. That sounded like Josh. But it couldn't be.

The RoboMe moved in closer. "It's me."

He picked up the toy and held the pixelated face closer. "Josh?"

The face smiled. "Yes, Andre. It's really me."

"But how?"

A man stepped into the doorway. "I did it."

Andre jumped and nearly dropped Josh. "Who... Who are you?"

The man smiled. "I'm Notch."

Andre looked from Notch to Josh. "He got you out of Minecraft?"

Notch moved into the room. "We don't have time to get into that right now. Where's Herobrine?"

Andre pointed to the closed pod. "He's in there."

The lines on Notch's forehead grew thicker. "Where did you send him?"

Andre handed Notch the yellow sticky note with the IP address.

Notch stared at it for a brief moment and then looked at the pod. "How long has he been in there?"

"About five minutes."

Notch looked around at the lab ceiling. "He's had about fifty years in there, and the world hasn't collapsed yet. Maybe we still have time."

Andre stood up from the chair. "Time for what?"

Notch looked at him. "The place you sent him was a world I created on top of the internet. After I failed to create an intelligent avatar by hand, I knew there was no shortcut to creating artificial life. So I designed a world that replicated our own in an attempt to allow avatars to create themselves and to evolve on their own from rudimentary logic programs to more realized thinkers.

"They were going to be the best artificial intelligent avatars ever created. They would eventually be included in the single player version of Minecraft to provide realism never before attained in a game by populating the randomly generated towns with living, breathing characters for the player to interact with. It was to be my greatest masterpiece."

A thought occurred to Andre. "If he just went

in five minutes ago, why did you say he's been in there for fifty years?"

Notch looked at him, a sadness filling his eyes. "I said there were no good shortcuts to creating intelligent life. But that doesn't mean I didn't try. I sped up the program clock so that the avatars would evolve faster. I didn't want to sit around and wait a thousand years in real time for them to become just as smart as we are. But I also didn't want to make it too fast, or I wouldn't be able to monitor their progress. For every minute of real time out here, the world in the program progresses ten years."

Andre looked at the pod, his heart beating faster. "Herobrine has been in that world for fifty years already?"

Notch nodded.

"What has he been doing in there all this time?"

"That world is connected to the internet at a fundamental level. Once inside, he can access any system connected to the internet in the real world."

"So, by going into that world, he can take over all the computers in our world?"

"Yes."

"Why did you do that?!"

Notch shrugged. "I needed the distributed processing power to make the world believable to the avatars inside."

Josh rolled forward. "How do we stop him?"

Notch looked down. "You would need to go into the world and stop him there. Now that he is inside, you can't stop him from out here."

Josh looked as serious as he could, with his cartoon pixelated face. "Then let's find a couple of computers and go stop him."

Notch shook his head again. "The system is running too fast. You would need to connect directly with the system at the brainwave level to keep up."

Andre pointed to the pod. "This pod is a one-of-a-kind."

A new voice intruded from the hallway. "What's a one-of-a-kind?"

They all turned to see Suzy standing in the doorway.

She cocked her head to one side. "What are you doing here?" She pointed at Notch. "And who is he?"

Andre rushed up to Suzy. "What are you doing here?"

She placed her hands on her hips. "I asked you first."

He looked back at Notch, who shrugged his shoulders indicating it was up to Andre to explain everything.

He looked back at Suzy. "Can you keep a secret?"

Chapter 10

Andre did his best to get Suzy caught up on everything, with Josh and Notch filling in the blanks. When he was done, she leaned down to look at Josh on the iPhone stuck to the top of the RoboMe.

"So you really are Josh stuck inside a Minecraft world inside this phone?"

Andre knelt down next to Josh and looked at her. "Yes. And Herobrine was the one who tried to pick a fight with you today."

She stood back up. "And the only way to stop him is to go into this new Minecraft world? Before he gains access to the computers in the real world and destroys humanity?"

Josh rolled back and forth. "That sounds about right."

"Can he really gain access to any computer in the world from inside the Minecraft world?"

Notch nodded. "If it's connected to the

internet, he can get onto it. Given enough time, he will control satellites, power stations, even nuclear missiles. The world is not safe as long as he is in there."

She smiled. "Then let's go."

Andre frowned. "Go? What are you talking about?"

"My dad's been working on a parallel project to yours, and he already has two brainwave helmets ready for testing. We can use those to go inside Minecraft. Since they communicate at the speed of thought, we should be able to keep up with the accelerated time."

Notch stepped closer. "I can't send you in too. It's risky enough sending Andre in. I don't want to put anyone else in jeopardy."

She turned on him. "Risky is sending those two yahoos in without me. This world, it's based on Minecraft, right?"

Notch nodded.

"I'm a better player than both of them

combined. You would be stupid to keep me out. Besides, they're my dad's brainwave helmets. If I can't go, nobody goes."

Andre grabbed her shoulders and looked her in the eyes. "The whole world is at stake here."

She gave him a hard stare back. "I know. And without me, you guys don't stand a chance."

Andre looked to Notch for support.

Notch shrugged his shoulders. "She's got a point. I can send Josh in directly using the phone, and there are two of you, and two helmets. If all three of you go, we stand a better chance of stopping him."

Josh rolled up to their feet and they all looked down at him. "Then it's settled. We all go in together."

Chapter 11

Notch finished connecting the helmets to Andre and Suzy. Josh was plugged into a port on the computer linked to the helmets.

He adjusted Andre's helmet one last time. "It's been ten minutes since Herobrine went into the pod, so he'll have a hundred year head start on his plan. Since none of you are default characters in the program, neither you nor Herobrine will age like the rest of the people in there."

He kept checking cables and connections as he continued his instructions. "Once you go through the portal, the only way back is with the crystal cube I gave Josh. The cube will not work unless all four of you, and that means Herobrine too, are touching it at the same time."

He pointed to a map he called up on the monitor. "I have put a copy of the world map in Josh's inventory and marked all the locations where Herobrine might be able to pierce the firewall and gain access to the real world. Every one of these places is represented as a major city in the program. To gain access to the firewall, he will need to breach the real walls of the city's inner hub. There are only seven inner hubs the world over, so that at least narrows down the places you will need to look for him."

He checked the screens that had full pages of text scrolling across it rapidly. "I won't be able to communicate with you once you are inside since time is accelerated."

He stopped checking the equipment and looked at Andre and Suzy. "Basically, once you pass through the portal, you are on your own."

Suzy shifted uncomfortably in her chair. "What happens if we die inside the program?"

"You'll wake up in the lab back here. I would try to avoid death as much as possible though. By the time I reset the system and send you back in, several decades would have elapsed. The good news is that, even if it takes you a thousand years to stop him, only a couple of hours will have passed in real time. Nobody will have the chance to miss any of you here before you return."

Andre looked up at him. "If we don't get old, then I guess we won't be dying anyway?"

Notch smiled. "I wouldn't worry too much about dying. I set your avatars with the highest health level I could. You can withstand a lot more damage, but you're not immortal, so be careful when confronting Herobrine; he will be as strong as you are. If anyone can hurt you in the program, he can. But you will heal quickly."

He sat down at the terminal and typed furiously into the command window before pausing with his hand over the enter key.

"Is everyone ready?"

All three replied at once. "Let's do this."

He looked at the three children he was sending to a dangerous world of his own creation. He had one last piece of advice that was more for the preservation of his world than it was for their protection.

"The people you'll meet do not know they are computer programs. Please don't tell them, even though I doubt they would believe you if you did. And I think it's best not to let them see how powerful you are. Think about how this world would react if superheroes actually showed up one day. You can expect a similar response from the beings in my world. And please, do your best not to interfere with their natural progression. Oh, and never let them see you fly."

Notch pressed down on the enter key.

Chapter 12

Josh felt a rush of energy at the same moment he thought he heard Notch mention they could fly.

Bright lights swirled around him, swooped away, and coalesced into defined pinpoint spots that became stars in the night sky. While it was nighttime, there was enough ambient light around that he could see he was standing in a field of grass. He lifted his arms up to see the square boxy hands of a Minecraft avatar.

Andre and Suzy materialized out of thin air right in front of him and looked at him before looking at each other.

They had made it. There were all inside.

In the middle of the field stood the portal, just as Notch said it would. The center of the portal shimmered with a purple hue, beckoning them in.

Josh felt the square lump of the crystal cube

inside the satchel hanging over his shoulder. In this world, they would not be using a magical floating menu system. If he had something in his inventory, it would be in the bag on his shoulder. Notch had created this world to model the real world, even if only a little.

He pulled out the crystal cube and inspected it by the glow of the portal. They were only able to leave by using the crystal cube. And all four of them would be needed to activate it.

Once they entered through the portal, they weren't going home until they found Herobrine.

Suzy reached her hands out to Josh and Andre. "Are we ready?"

Josh and Andre looked at each other and then took hold of Suzy's outstretched hands.

Together, the three of them stepped through the portal into a world both familiar, and unfamiliar.

Chapter 13

Night turned instantly into day.

They were still in the same field, but the portal was gone; and it was now the middle of the day instead of the middle of the night.

A scream in the distance made them all turn at once.

A young boy, surrounded by a flock of sheep, screamed, "It's Him!" dropped his staff and ran away. Some of the sheep, startled by the sudden outburst of their protector, bolted into the center of the flock. This triggered the rest of the flock to react in a blind panic, and soon, sheep ran bleating in every direction.

Suzy turned to Josh. "So much for not scaring the natives."

Andre watched the young shepherd crest a nearby hill and disappear again over the other side without looking back. "What do you think he saw?"

Josh shook his head. "Only us appearing out of nowhere in the middle of an empty field."

Suzy watched the sheep calm down and resuming eating grass where they stopped. "Do you think Herobrine appeared the same way?"

Andre shook his head. "That would have been a hundred years ago. Even if he popped up in the middle of a busy city, nobody today would remember that."

Suzy nodded. "Actually, it's something to check in to. We can see if there are any legends of a superhuman appearing in this same field."

Josh looked around at the low rolling hills in every direction. "Which way do we go?"

Suzy pointed in the direction the boy had run. The majority of the flock had started moving in the same direction. "We follow the sheep."

Chapter 14

Sheep don't move too fast on their own without a shepherd to guide them. And they stop far too often to snack on grass and weeds. The sun was nearing the horizon by the time the three of them saw the first signs of civilization.

Andre crouched next to a small stream that ran parallel to the road the sheep had led them to. "I should be thirsty by now, but I feel fine."

Josh thought about his own stomach. It didn't feel empty. It didn't feel full either. He just didn't notice anything about it. "I guess we don't have to eat or drink to stay alive."

Suzy was carrying a baby lamb in her arms that had been struggling to keep up, despite how slow they were moving. "That's good, 'cause we don't have money for food anyway. Being a Minecraft world, I guess we can build a shelter out of dirt if we need to."

Andre stood up from the creek. "Do you

think we need to sleep?"

Josh raised his hands, palm side up, and shrugged his shoulders in an "I don't know" gesture. "I don't feel tired, and we've been walking for hours."

Suzy set the baby lamb down and it ran to catch up with its mother. "I guess that's the price of immortality. No eating, drinking, or sleeping."

They continued walking along the road, past one farmhouse after another, until they saw a four-story stone wall surrounding a large city ahead of them.

It was the middle of the day, and the city gates were wide open. They strode in through the gates of the city and headed for the center of town. If they were going to find someone to ask about ancient legends from a hundred years ago, the center of town was the best place to start.

As they walked, villagers crossed to the opposite side of the street or turned around to walk back the way they came. No one approached them or even looked at them directly. It seemed that everyone was afraid of the newcomers.

Andre leaned over as they walked and whispered. "Not too friendly, are they?"

Suzy smiled at a group of children who had stopped their game of kick-the-block to watch the trio pass by. As soon as she said "Hello" they scattered and disappeared into several doorways.

Josh looked up and smiled at a little boy watching him from a second story window. The boy's mother appeared, pulled him back, and quickly closed the shutters.

Josh shook his head. "Yeah. Not friendly at all."

A commanding voice cut through the silence behind them. "Stop right there!"

They turned around and faced twenty armed soldiers, all pointing their drawn bows at them.

Chapter 15

All three of them shot their arms up to the sky. The leader of the soldiers, the only one not pointing a bow and arrow at them, walked forward.

"What is your business here?"

Suzy stepped forward one step, the soldiers immediately repositioning their bows to point exclusively at her.

"We come in peace."

The leader regarded her with a frown. "The last time someone said that, it took nearly a decade to rebuild the city."

Andre joined her, the soldiers switching their aim back and forth between the two who had stepped forward. "We are not like the one who came before."

"What do you know of the one who came before?"

Suzy and Andre looked at each other.

"I guess a hundred years is not long enough to forget someone like Herobrine," Suzy said.

At the utterance of his name, the soldiers became agitated and quickly shifted their aim between all three of them as if they didn't know who to shoot first.

The leader stepped forward even closer. "We dare not speak his name. What do you want with Him?"

Josh stepped up to join his two friends. "We came to stop Him."

The air grew tense as the leader sized up the trio, before breaking out into a wide grin. He motioned to the soldiers to lower their weapons. They complied and all dropped to one knee, bowing to the trio. The leader stepped closer to them and bowed low in front of them. "My name is Lord Franco, and we are at your service."

Chapter 16

As soon as the sun set, the gates to the city were closed and locked.

Lord Franco led the trio around the city and introduced them to everyone they saw. As they walked, he filled them in on the stories told by their ancestors about what had taken place five generations before near his city.

"When word came that a stranger had appeared in the grazing fields far to the north, my ancestors welcomed Him at first. Then the stranger destroyed the city with his bare hands. He tore down the walls block by block. Walls that had stood for a thousand years, protecting our forefathers from numerous invaders. They quickly learned nothing would protect them from Him.

"Our ancestors tried everything to stop Him. Swords, arrows, fire, even dynamite. At first, they thought the dynamite had finally killed Him, but then he arose and wiped the town off the map before he left."

Josh listened intently, focusing on everything Lord Franco said until he had a question. "Where did he go?"

Lord Franco exhaled slowly before answering. "For the longest time, he sat in the field where he first appeared. It was as if he were waiting for something." He looked at the trio. "Or someone."

Suzy's forehead wrinkled as she thought of something. "How long did he stay there?"

"He sat in that field for two generations. He never ate, he never slept, he never aged. My great-grandparents spent most of their lives hiding in caves; only coming out in small groups to scavenge for food. They barely survived. And then one day, the scouts reported that he was gone. They watched the field for over a year, but he never returned.

"Slowly, my grandparents came out of hiding

and rebuilt our city with even bigger walls. There were many enemies who came to attack us, but our stronger city repelled them all. They started the practice of using the field for grazing so that they could keep a watchful eye on it daily.

"When nothing happened for generations, the stories became more legend than fact. Wild stories told by our elders as a warning to never become complacent. The stories we grew up with were mere lessons. They were no longer believed to be based on true historical accounts."

He looked at them. "And then you appeared in the same spot; a hundred years later."

Josh remembered the map Notch had given them. He pulled it out of his satchel and unfolded it. He held it up for Lord Franco to see.

"Where are we on this map?"

Lord Franco took it and inspected it, turning it this way and that. "What is this map of?"

"The world."

"What part of the world?"

"The whole world."

He gave Josh a surprised look and laughed. "Don't be ridiculous. The world is flat and this map shows it as an expanded cube, with multiple sides. You might want to check your source."

Suzy took the map and folded it back up. "How far have you traveled?"

Lord Franco waved his arms around the city. "I have lived here my entire life."

"Have any of you traveled?"

He laughed again. "Why would we? We have everything we need here, safe inside these walls."

Andre spoke up. "Do you know anyone who has traveled?"

Lord Franco ran a hand over his face and puffed his cheeks with air. "You might try the trading cities to the east. They are port cities and have travelers from all over pass through them. But they'll tell you the same thing. The world is flat. If you're lucky, you might meet someone who has been to the edge of the world."

Chapter 17

After Lord Franco gave them a tour of the town, he set them up for the night in the inn by the front gates. They didn't feel sleepy, so instead, they planned their next move.

Josh spread the map on the table and pointed to a small dot at the base of a mountain range. "I ran into a local trade merchant in the market. According to him, we are right about here. I say we head for the port cities to the east."

Andre pointed at the closest marked city to the north. "Notch said Herobrine would try to get to the outside world from one of the hubs in these cities. I say we go for the closest one and hope he's still there."

This started an argument; something that the twin brothers had plenty of experience in.

Suzy got between them and pushed them apart. "If we want to stop Herobrine, we have to work together. And we can't do that if you two are fighting all the time."

Andre nodded. "She's right. And she can be our tie-breaker. Where do you think we should go first, Suzy? Should we try to find Herobrine at the next hub, or do we waste our time talking to the natives in the wrong direction?"

Josh pushed against Suzy's hands as she still held them apart. "That's not fair. His idea is just as stupid as mine."

Suzy struggled to keep them apart. "Well, at least we agree that both ideas are equally stupid."

The brothers stopped pushing and turned on her. "Hey!" they both said simultaneously.

She smiled. "And both ideas are equally brilliant. We have nothing to go on except what Notch and Lord Franco have said. And neither of them knows where Herobrine is at this very moment. Since nobody knows where he is, no place is any worse than the other."

Josh looked at his brother, and then back to her. "So what do we do?"

Andre held up his fist and placed it into the flat of his palm. "Rock-paper-scissors?"

Chapter 18

Lord Franco stood at the top of the hill overlooking the valley that would take the three newcomers away from his city. The wind lifted the edge of his cloak and he gripped it tight against the chilly air.

"Are you sure you don't want to stay a while longer? I would love to know where you are from."

Josh smiled. "Sorry Lord Franco. I'm afraid, for the safety of you and your city, where we come from must remain a secret."

Lord Franco looked back at the city that was his responsibility. "Do you think you can stop Him?"

Andre nodded. "We are going to do everything we can to take Him back to our world."

Suzy placed a hand on Lord Franco's arm. "We won't stop trying until we do."

Lord Franco smiled at her. "Feel free to tell anyone you meet that you grew up here in Mallowholt. I will vouch for you should anyone come around asking questions."

They took turns shaking his hand and then mounted their horses, a gift for each of them from Lord Franco. Josh pulled up on the reins to keep his spirited horse under control. "Thank you Lord Franco, for all your help. And for the horses."

Lord Franco smiled. "It's the least I can do for the saviors of our land. So tell me, where are you headed?"

Josh looked at Andre and smiled. "We're headed for the first hub. Maybe we'll get lucky and Herobr..."

Lord Franco cut him off. "Never speak his name aloud."

"Maybe... He will be there."

Lord Franco frowned. "What if he's not?"

Suzy pulled her horse close to Lord Franco.

"Wherever he is, we will find him."

Together, the three of them pulled on their reins, kicked their horses into a full gallop, and rode away from the first town of many they would be visiting on their quest.

The Adventure Continues...
Episode 2: Day of the Creepers

Available December 16, 2013

Tell your friends to catch up on all the available episodes so you can discuss what you think will happen next!

S.D. Stuart's Minecraft Adventures Series

SEASON ONE RELEASE SCHEDULE

Herobrine Rises (Ep. 0 - 12/2/2013)

The Portal (Ep. 1 - 12/9/2013)

Day of the Creepers (Ep. 2 - 12/16/2013)

Here Be Dragons (Ep. 3 - 1/6/2014)

The Dark Temple (Ep. 4 - 1/13/2014)

Immortal Zombie (Ep. 5 - 1/20/2014)

Displaced Kingdom (Ep. 6 - 1/27/2014)

Forgotten Reboot (Ep. 7 - 2/3/2014)

Wither's Destruction (Ep. 8 - 2/10/2014)

Also by Steve DeWinter

Inherit The Throne

The Warrior's Code

The Red Cell Report (COMING SOON)

Written as S.D. Stuart

The Wizard of OZ: A Steampunk Adventure

The Scarecrow of OZ: A Steampunk Adventure

Fugue: The Cure

Herobrine Rises: A Minecraft Adventure

Made in the USA
San Bernardino, CA
23 March 2014